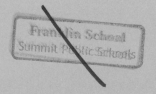

SYDNEY & SIMON
GO GREEN!

STORY BY PAUL A. REYNOLDS   ART BY PETER H. REYNOLDS

ini Charlesbridge

To my son Joshua Keith Reynolds whose compassion and love for the environment has inspired me—and many others—to go green
—P. A. R.

To Margie Leonard, true blue with a heart of gold
—P. H. R.

Text copyright © 2015 by Paul A. Reynolds
Illustrations copyright © 2015 by Peter H. Reynolds
All rights reserved, including the right of reproduction in whole or in part in any form.
Charlesbridge and colophon are registered trademarks of Charlesbridge Publishing, Inc.

Published by Charlesbridge
85 Main Street
Watertown, MA 02472
(617) 926-0329
www.charlesbridge.com

Library of Congress Cataloging-in-Publication Data
Reynolds, Paul A.
    Sydney & Simon: go green!/written by Paul A. Reynolds; illustrated by Peter H. Reynolds.
        p. cm.
    Summary: After discovering that a green sea turtle was harmed by plastic in the ocean, twin mice Sydney and Simon come up with a creative campaign to increase recycling and reduce the amount of trash created in their home, school, and town.
    ISBN 978-1-58089-677-1 (reinforced for library use)
    ISBN 978-1-60734-913-6 (ebook)
    ISBN 978-1-60734-694-4 (ebook pdf)
1. Pollution—Juvenile fiction. 2. Recycling (Waste, etc.)—Juvenile fiction.
3. Twins—Juvenile fiction. 4. Music—Juvenile fiction. 5. Critical thinking—Juvenile fiction. [1. Environmental protection—Fiction. 2. Recycling (Waste)—Fiction. 3. Green movement—Fiction. 4. Twins—Fiction. 5. Music—Fiction.
6. Mice—Fiction.] I. Reynolds, Peter, 1961- illustrator. II. Title. III. Title: Sydney and Simon. IV. Title: Go green!
PZ7.R337643Sy 2015
813.54—dc23
[E] 2014036260

Printed in China
(hc) 10 9 8 7 6 5 4 3 2 1

Illustrations created with ink, watercolor wash, water, and tea
Display type set in Chowderhead by Font Diner
Text typeset in Schneidler BT by Bitstream Inc.
Color separations by Colourscan Print Co Pte Ltd, Singapore
Printed by 1010 Printing International Limited in Huizhou, Guangdong, China
Production supervision by Brian G. Walker
Reynolds Studio supervision by Julia Anne Young
Designed by Diane M. Earley

Contents

1

Turtle Troubles!

It was field-trip day, and Sydney Starr could not believe that she was staring at a real, living, swimming green sea turtle.

Dr. Romano, the veterinarian at Wonder Falls Aquarium, had rescued the sea turtle and named her Greenie. After eating plastic garbage in the ocean, Greenie had become sick.

"Dr. Romano says you will get better here," Sydney told her new friend. But Sydney felt uneasy thinking about trash hurting sea creatures.

Later that day Sydney and her twin brother walked home from school. "Earth to Simon! Can you hear me? The green sea turtles need our help," Sydney said.

"Can this wait, Syd?" asked Simon. "I'm listening to a really cool song on DJ K's radio station."

"No, this is a big problem that needs serious *thinkering*," Sydney said.

"Dr. Romano is already taking care of Greenie. There's nothing we can do to help," Simon said.

"*Nothing* we can do? Guess who makes all this garbage?" Sydney asked. She pointed to trash cans piled high. "We all do."

"That stinks!" Simon exclaimed.

"You're right it stinks," said Sydney.

"No, I mean those trash cans really smell," Simon said.

"Seriously, Simon," Sydney begged. "The more trash we make, the more there's a chance that some of that trash could end up in the ocean."

"Hold on, Miss Sydney Starr. I never litter. I use trash cans," Simon argued.

"But a trash can," Sydney said, "is a trash *can't*. It can't just make trash disappear."

Sydney took out the sketch she made at the aquarium. Her art showed how garbage can get blown, swept, or thrown into sewers, streams, and rivers. Eventually it can end up going all the way to the ocean. That's where animals try to eat it or get tangled in it.

Simon didn't look convinced.

Just as the twins reached their front door, their dad came running out holding a big box of plastic bottles. "Excuse me, kids, trash coming through!" he said. Clearly Mr. Starr had been drinking a lot of bottled water while writing his new science poetry book.

Sydney's whiskers always wiggled when she was worried. They were *really* wiggly now. "You see? This is evidence that our own family is part of the problem," she said.

TRASH TRACKER
PLASTIC
PAPER
ELECTRONIC
FOOD WASTE
OTHER
M
T
W
TH
F
S
S

2

Trash Trackers

Sydney scurried inside with her Wonder Journal. She opened it up and started drawing a chart. "I'm starting the Starr Family Trash Tracker Mission," she told Simon.

"Trash Tracker?" Simon asked.

"Yup!" Sydney said. "We'll see how much trash our family makes in a week by observing and collecting data."

Simon had a hard time believing that his family was creating too much trash. But there was no stopping Sydney. So he decided he might as well help her.

For the next week Sydney and Simon tracked the amount of their family's trash leaving the apartment building.

On Monday Sydney spotted her dad carrying out *even more* plastic bottles! She made a note in her Wonder Journal.

MONDAY

On Tuesday Mr. and Mrs. Starr put an old chair and the twins' rickety tricycles outside for the garbage truck. "Maybe we don't want these things anymore, but someone else could reuse them," Simon recorded in his Wonder Journal on his tablet.

When Wednesday came, Mrs. Starr packed the family's lunches in paper bags, with plastic spoons, plastic sandwich bags, and paper napkins. Sydney wrote, "Yikes! All that will be trash by noontime!"

By the time Thursday rolled around, the Dumpster behind their apartment was overflowing with trash from their neighbor Myra Foxton's sixteenth birthday party. Simon made a voice recording. "Trash Tracker Update, this is Garbologist Simon Starr reporting: We've got a mountain of boxes and wrapping paper heading for the Wonder Falls dump!"

On Friday Simon got a box in the mail. It was filled with bubble wrap and a smaller box. Inside that box was a plastic package. Inside that was another package. It held four strings for Simon's ukulele. He dumped all the packaging in the trash.

Sydney gasped.

Simon blushed. "Sorry, Syd. I guess even *I'm* part of the problem."

Sydney sighed. "I hate to say it, but there might be another place where trash is a problem."

3

The Trash Adds Up

Sydney seemed pretty sure there were more trash troubles at Wonder Falls Elementary. She asked their best friend, Finn Finster, and Mrs. Jarrett, the lunch lady, to help investigate.

Together they tallied the number of plastic spoons, bags, and bottles; food; and recyclable papers that were being thrown away.

Each day the school custodian, Mr. Clutterbuck, helped them weigh the trash on a big scale. They wanted to know exactly how much was being tossed out.

Finn thought the school should be sending all that paper and plastic to a recycling collection facility. That way it could be made into new plastic and paper products.

After a few weeks, Sydney, Simon, and Finn had shocking news to share in Mr. Gorgonzola's math class.

Their charts and equations showed that the students and teachers were producing about three hundred pounds of trash every day.

Finn passed two bricks around the class. "This means," Finn explained, "that each of us makes ten pounds of garbage a week. That is how much two bricks weigh. Heavy, right?!"

Mr. Gorgonzola loved that his class was getting to see, hear, and even feel how big the problem really was.

After school Simon admitted he was beginning to understand the problem. "The more trash our family, neighborhood, and school make," he said, "the greater chance that trash could end up in Greenie's ocean home."

"Exactly. So how can we get everyone to pay attention and cut down on all the garbage?" Sydney asked.

"I'm not sure how we'll do it," Simon said, "but let's remember what Mom always says: *Creative problem solvers never give up!*"

4

An Artful Solution

The next day Sydney and Simon were in their favorite place in the entire school: the STEAM Studio. This was where Ms. Fractalini inspired students to discover the ways Science, Technology, Engineering, Arts, and Math connect to make the world a better place.

"Sydney and Simon, Mr. Gorgonzola told me about your math-tastic trash tally and your concern for Greenie," Ms. Fractalini said. "Let's put our heads together and build something to help us consider the problem of too much trash."

The class was ready for some creative collaboration. The students shared dozens of ideas and sketched plenty of plans. In the end, they decided to recycle and make a huge sculpture of a sea turtle.

What did they use for building supplies? Trash, of course! Plastic water bottles, old cardboard, plastic bags, and used milk cartons became the building blocks of their masterpiece.

All the while, Sydney shared some trash trivia.

"Over one trillion plastic bags and bottles are used all over the world every day," she said. "Some of them end up in the ocean. Poor Greenie thought a piece of plastic was food," she explained.

"Does anyone remember why plastic is not very biodegradable?" Ms. Fractalini asked.

Finn rushed to answer. "I've got this, Ms. F," he said.

Finn sketched cartoons on the whiteboard as he spoke.

"Plastic is not very biodegradable because bacteria don't like to eat plastic," Finn said. He explained how matter—solids, liquids, and gases—are made of atoms. Atoms are the smallest part of every object in the world. Some atoms allow bacteria to eat through them in a few weeks or a year. But plastic's atoms are linked in a way that doesn't let bacteria do their job very well.

"That's why it can take anywhere from four hundred and fifty years to one thousand years for a plastic bottle to decompose," he added.

Finn remembered all this from an experiment the class did last fall. They had buried a paper bag, a cloth bag, and plastic bag. After six weeks the plastic bag was the only thing that hadn't started decomposing.

Ms. Fractalini was impressed by Finn's explanation and drawings. "Finn, you and this wonderful, STEAM-powered sculpture are making us think a lot about the effects of trash on our environment," she said.

"Mixing science and art is music to my ears," Simon offered.

"That's it!" Sydney cried. Simon had given her another idea.

5

Jingles & Junk

Back at home Sydney told Simon her big idea. "Let's do another kind of smart art," she said. "Let's write and sing a song to get everyone to go green."

"Go green?" asked Simon. "I only *go green* when I'm feeling seasick on a boat."

Sydney laughed. She explained that going green means doing things to make our environment a better place.

The twins got to work in what Simon liked to call his Musical Media MegaStudio. Sydney called it his bedroom. After hours and hours of writing and playing, they had the perfect song.

They sang it for their parents.

LET'S GO GREEN!
(sing to the tune of THIS LAND IS YOUR LAND) ← BY WOODY GUTHRIE

This trash is your trash, this trash is my trash,
from plastic store bags, to the junk we toss fast.
From candy wrappers, to the needless garbage heaps.
Let's go green now, you and me!

It's time we go green, to save the oceans.
Trash caught in streams is just trash in motion.
It keeps on floating, out to the blue, blue sea.
Let's get recycling, you and me!

Let's be more careful with what we do use.
Some thrifty thinking can help us reduce.
The more we reuse, the less there'll be. (you'll see!)
Let's get recycling, you and me!

This trash is your trash, this trash is my trash,
from plastic store bags, to the junk we toss fast.
From candy wrappers, to the needless garbage heaps.
LET'S GO GREEN NOW, YOU AND ME!

Lyrics by Simon & Sydney

"You have invented a musical way to spread a message that matters! Bravo!" exclaimed Mrs. Starr.

Simon raised his hands to stop the cheering. "I'm glad you like the song, but I want to make it even greener," he said. "And not by writing it down in green magic marker, either."

"What if we make musical instruments from things we find at the trash dump?" Simon asked.

Sydney's eyes lit up. "Wow, if we could do that, our music would be super green!"

She and Simon grabbed their skateboards and headed for the junkyard.

When Sydney and Simon arrived at Mouselmore's
junkyard and thrift shop, they were greeted by
Mr. Mac Mouselmore.

Simon asked if they could use some of the
things in his shop and the dump to make musical
instruments.

Mr. Mouselmore grinned. "Of course! It's fun
to rescue rubbish," he said. "As I always say:
One mouse's trash is another mouse's treasure!"

The twins spent all afternoon engineering their junkyard instruments. First they imagined the possibilities. They talked about their ideas, gathered materials, sketched plans, and started building. Some plans didn't work the first time, so they improved their designs and tried again.

In the end Simon used an old board, nails, and some wires from a broom to make a guitar.

Sydney created a percussion station with old pots and pans and plastic pipes.

6
Tuning In

At home the twins went straight to the music studio. They played their newly recycled instruments and recorded their song with Simon's computer.

Eventually Simon sent their recording and a note about Greenie to DJ Kurt Koostow at their favorite radio station. If DJ K liked the song, he might play it for everyone in Wonder Falls.

"Sydney, just so you know, DJ K is *very* picky about the music he plays," Simon said. "Don't be too sad if he doesn't like our song."

"I'll just be sad for Greenie," Sydney said. "That sweet turtle is depending on us."

Then they waited. And waited.

One week later, just when Sydney was losing hope, the phone rang. She answered and immediately recognized the voice on the other end.

"Hi, there," the voice said. "It's DJ K here from Wonder Falls Radio. I'm looking for Sydney and Simon. Their song is seriously awesome!"

Sydney was stunned. She couldn't even respond. She quickly handed the phone to Simon. "It's DJ K," Sydney squeaked. "He . . . he . . . he likes our song!"

Simon grabbed the phone. "That's great DJ K!
Will you play it on your station?" he asked.

DJ K chuckled. "Listen to my show right now,"
he said. Simon had the Wonder Falls Radio app on
his tablet. Within seconds the twins could hear
their song streaming live. Sydney let out a squeal.

When the song finished, DJ K spoke to his
listeners. "Did you hear that, my Wonder Falls
fans? Let's all do what this song says. Let's go green
for Sydney and Simon, for Greenie the sea turtle
and her ocean friends, and for Mother Earth!"

DJ K played "Let's Go Green!" all week long.

The next Monday the twins stopped by the neighborhood cheese shop. Mrs. Asiago was excited to see them. "Sydney and Simon! I danced to your new song this morning when I heard it on the radio."

"Wow! You heard it?" they asked.

"I sure did. It inspired me to reuse these old chairs from Mr. Mouselmore's junkyard, rather than buy new ones," said Mrs. Asiago.

The twins' smiles got even bigger. "It's working," Sydney cheered.

On Tuesday Blake Feldspar greeted them on the playground. Big Blake was usually in a bad mood. He never paid attention to the twins.

"Hey, Double S!" he called to Sydney and Simon. "I heard your song on the radio. You actually know DJ K?" Blake asked.

"Yup!" Sydney and Simon answered together.

"Cool! Count me in to help your turtles," said Blake. "From now on I'm not buying soda with those plastic ring holders anymore."

Double S did a double take. Did Blake just say he'd help? If he liked going green, then could the rest of Wonder Falls be far behind?

On Wednesday Mr. Starr showed off his new metal water bottle. "No more plastic bottles for me. I'm going to reuse this and refill it with tap water," he said proudly.

Mrs. Starr had bought everyone canvas lunch bags and cloth napkins. "Your song inspired me. Good-bye, plastic. Good-bye, paper. We make less trash when we wash and reuse things," she announced.

Sydney and Simon were very pleased. Could they really get everyone going green?

That Thursday Mrs. Jarrett the lunch lady launched the new "Go Green" cafeteria program that she had been planning. Students would now put food scraps in a compost bin instead of trash barrels. Decomposed compost would be used to fertilize the school's vegetable garden.

"Say good-bye to plastic forks and spoons," said Mrs. Jarrett. "And say hello to reusable metal silverware." The best part about it all? Milk and juice containers and cardboard boxes were being saved and reused for art projects.

All the while Mrs. Jarrett kept singing the twins' song.

Finally, on Friday, the twins ran into Mr. Gorgonzola.

"Sydney and Simon, I love your song! I've been listening to it all week. And look here! Calculations show that the school is already reducing its trash output."

The twins thought this was green-tastic.

Everywhere they looked, Wonder Falls was recycling, reusing, and making less trash.

Sydney and Simon decided to celebrate the good news with Greenie.

Dr. Romano was thrilled to see the twins arrive at the aquarium. "Soon Greenie will be released back into the ocean," she told them. "That little sea turtle has been doing really well, especially since I've been playing her this new song." Dr. Romano turned on her radio.

"Hey!" Sydney squealed. "That's *our* song!"

Greenie did a double flip underwater.

"Greenie, if we all make more creative choices about how we deal with trash," Sydney said, "then maybe there will be less of a chance for that garbage to pollute your home."

"You're right," said Simon. "We won't stop until we get everyone to . . ."

Glossary

app—an application, usually a small, specialized program (such as a game or radio station) made specifically for smartphones or computer tablets

art—something (such as a painting, drawing, song, or sculpture) that is created with imagination, is beautiful, or that shows important ideas or feelings

atom—the basic building block of all matter and the tiniest particle of a substance

bacteria—living things that are so small they cannot be seen with the naked eye; they live in soil, water, or the bodies of plants and animals and are important because of their chemical effects on other living things

biodegradable—capable of being destroyed slowly and broken down into very small parts by bacteria or other natural processes

compost—a mixture of decomposing matter of once living things (such as grass or fruit peels) that can be used to fertilize land

data—facts that can be used in planning, reasoning, or calculating

decompose—to break down through chemical change

engineering—the work of creating and designing structures (such as bridges or pipes) by engineers or any person who applies science and math to make such structures

environment—the natural world and the conditions that influence the ability to survive in the natural world

evidence—a sign that shows something is true

fertilize—to make soil or land richer for plant growth by adding chemicals or a natural substance, such as compost

going green—being friendly to the natural environment and looking to preserve and protect Earth's resources and living things

junkyard—a place where you can buy, sell, or leave things that have been thrown away or have little value

litter—to carelessly discard trash

math—the science of numbers, shapes, and quantities and the relation among them

matter—anything that takes up space and is often classified into three main states: solids, liquids, and gases; under certain conditions, matter can change between different states

media studio—a room where an artist (such as a singer, photographer, or sculptor) works on a particular form of art

percussion—musical instruments (such as drums, xylophones, or cymbals) that are played by hitting or shaking

plastic—a man-made material that can be molded into shapes while soft and then set into a more rigid form; usually made from a combination of chemical methods

recycle—to make something new from something that has been used before

science—information about or the study of the natural world based on facts learned through observations and experiments

streaming—steady, continuous flow or playing of a video or song on a computer or technological device

technology—the use of science in industry or engineering to help solve or invent useful things; a machine or piece of equipment that is made by technology, such as a computer tablet

thinkering—Sydney's word for a combination of "thinking" and "tinkering" when using your imagination, experimenting, or searching for answers

thrift shop—a store that sells used goods

ukulele—a musical instrument that is similar to a small guitar with four strings

veterinarian—a person who is trained to give medical care to animals

How Green Is Your STEAM?

Dear Readers,

Did you know that we are twins, like Sydney and Simon? Just like these clever, creative mice, we use our double-powered twinergy to help make our earth cleaner and greener.

In fact, we helped celebrate the very first Earth Day on April 22, 1970! We were only nine years old, but that didn't stop us from using our smarts, arts, and hearts to pick up trash and make anti-littering posters. Now that we're grown-ups, we still pick up litter. We also now drive hybrid electric cars and team up with our families to recycle and reuse.

Because we are as curious as Sydney and Simon, we're huge fans of using the STEAM approach to find ways to make the world cleaner and greener. STEAM stands for Science, Technology, Engineering, Arts, and Math. STEAM thinkers are problem solvers who look for creative connections and breakthrough ideas across all these subjects. We used the Arts to write and illustrate this book as a way to inspire others to tackle the problems of ocean pollution and too much trash. Imagine if we all used STEAM thinking to make small changes in our environment. We are certain that we could make big changes together!

If you're a Green STEAM Thinker, you care about the environment in your school, home, community, nation, and world. Maybe you will inspire others by creating recycled school projects or gifts so extra materials don't get tossed in the dump. Maybe one day you'll invent a new substance that is more biodegradable than plastic. You might create a solar-powered scooter. Or perhaps you'll make art that reminds people that the earth doesn't have unlimited space for all the trash we're making. Every creative idea, every invention, and every artful message will help the world GO GREEN.

We hope Sydney and Simon's story inspires you to take action. Let us know how you plan to GO GREEN!